This Little Tiger book belongs to:

_____

_____

_____

For Tom ~ D B

For Lisa, Tony, and their little bears
Morgan and Macy ~ C P

LITTLE TIGER PRESS
An imprint of Magi Publications
1 The Coda Centre, 189 Munster Road, London SW6 6AW
www.littletigerpress.com

First published in Great Britain 2008
This edition published 2009

A CIP catalogue record for this book is available
from the British Library

Printed in China

2 4 6 8 10 9 7 5 3 1

Little Bear's Big Jumper

David Bedford Caroline Pedler

LITTLE TIGER PRESS
London

Big Bear loved his stripy jumper. It was warm. It was soft. And it was his very favourite.

But it was getting harder and harder to put on.

"It's too small for you!" said Little Bear, giggling.

"It's not," said Big Bear. "It fits just right!"

Mum laughed. "I think it's time I knitted you a new jumper, Big Bear. Why don't you give that one to your brother?"

"But it's too big
for him," said
Big Bear.
"No it's not,"
said Little Bear.

He pulled it quickly
over his head.
"It fits just right!"

"You'd better look after it,"
said Big Bear. "It's my
favourite jumper – EVER."
"I will," said Little Bear,
happily. "It's my favourite
ever too!"

Off they ran together to play. "Now I look just like you!" cried Little Bear.

Big Bear gave his
brother a piggyback
through the tall
grass. Little Bear
chuckled as he
was jiggled about.

The two brothers
jumped through the
puddles with a
Splish!
Splash!
Splosh!
"This is fun!" said
Big Bear.

Then Big Bear climbed along a high branch. "I'm climbing too!" said Little Bear. "You're pulling me down," cried his brother. "Get off!"

"I can wibble-wobble like you!" said Little Bear. "Stop it!" said Big Bear. "You're wobbling too much!"
And suddenly . . .

... **Crac*k!*** went the log,
as it split in two.
Sploos*h!*

went the bears as they landed
in a muddy puddle.

"Look what you've done!" yelled Big Bear. "You've broken the wobbly log. And you've made a mess of MY jumper!"

Little Bear looked down at
the soggy jumper. His lip
began to tremble.

"I'm s-o-r-r-y!" he said,
and he ran away into the
woods.

"Good then," said Big Bear,
grumpily. "It's better playing
on my own."

Big Bear slid down the slippery-slidey slope. He chased a butterfly until he was dizzy. Then he sat on the end of the see-saw. But with only one bear, it wouldn't go up or down.

Playing is no fun
without Little Bear,
he thought. And he
began to feel very
lonely.
   "Where ARE you,
Little Bear?"

Big Bear searched
the places Little Bear
liked the most. He
looked everywhere.
But he wasn't
in the hollow
honey tree . . .

or in their den
in the bush . . .

He wasn't even hiding under
the big rock.
Little Bear wasn't anywhere!
Where could he have
got to, all on
his own?

Suddenly, Big Bear saw a woolly thread. So he followed it quickly through the trees, round a bush and deeper and deeper into the woods, until at last he found . . .

. . . a very sad and
lonely Little Bear.

"I've ruined our favourite
ever jumper!" Little Bear
cried when he saw him.

Big Bear gave his brother a big hug. "Don't worry," he said, kindly. "It's only a jumper! I'm sorry I shouted at you."

"It's all right," Little Bear sniffed. "I shouldn't have run off without you."

Big Bear took him by the hand. "Let's go home," he said.

On the way back,
Big Bear wrapped
up all the wool
into a ball.

"We had a little accident,"
he told Mum when they
got home.
   "Poor Little Bear!"
said Mum. "Don't worry,
I know just what to do."

The very next morning,
Big Bear and Little Bear
had the best surprise . . .
two brand new, matching,
stripy jumpers!

"Now I can be just like
you, Little Bear!" said
Big Bear. "You're the best
brother EVER!"

Try these other *Little Tiger* titles for a perfect fit!

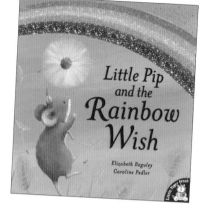

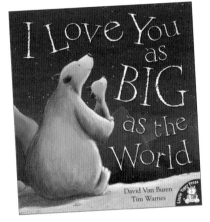

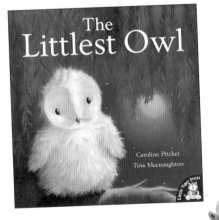

For information regarding any of the above titles
or for our catalogue, please contact us:
Little Tiger Press, 1 The Coda Centre,
189 Munster Road, London SW6 6AW
Tel: 020 7385 6333 Fax: 020 7385 7333
E-mail: info@littletiger.co.uk
www.littletigerpress.com